JACLYN KEARNEY

Noah's First Ark
Copyright © 2015 by Author Name. All rights reserved.
First Edition: September 2015

Contact information: Blackrose@nycap.rr.com
Web page: www.jaclyntracey.com
Blogspot: www.edensblackrose.blogspot.com
Cover work and all illustrations created by Elayne Griffith
Website: http://www.elaynegriffith.com

ISBN # 978-0-9967475-0-9

No part of this book may be reproduced, scanned, or distributed in any printed or electronic form without permission. Please do not participate in or encourage piracy of copyrighted materials in violation of the author's rights. Thank you for respecting the hard work of this author.

This is a work of fiction. Names, characters, places, and incidents either are the product of the author's imagination or are used fictitiously, and any resemblance to locales, events, business establishments, or actual persons—living or dead—is entirely coincidental.

Harper,

Hope you enjoy reading this. Your grandmother is one awesome lady too

Jacky Tracey

DEDICATION:

TO THE LITTLE MAN WHO GAVE ME THE BIGGEST SMILE.

WELCOME TO OUR FAMILY, NOAH RICHARD.

GRANDMA LOVES YOU MORE.

FOREVER!!!

IN A QUAINT TINY VILLAGE,
NOT SO VERY FAR AWAY,
STOOD A MAGNIFICENT CASTLE MADE OF SAND AND CLAY,
WHERE EVERY SATURDAY THE STAFF OFFERED,
PARFAITS AND TUTTI-FRUTTI SORBETS...
ALONG WITH TOOTHBRUSHES,
SO NO ONE WOULD GET TOOTH DECAY.

IN THE HOME LIVED A SILLY LITTLE QUEEN,
NOT A BONE IN HER BODY WAS MEAN.
A BRILLIANT SMILE WAS ALWAYS SEEN.
HER EYES WERE THE BLUEST OF BLUE,
AND ABOUT HER TATTOO ~
YES IT IS TRUE,
THERE WAS MUCH HULLABALOO,
OF A HOPPING KANGAROO,
WEARING HIGH-HEELED SHOES.
THE QUEEN ADORED IT...
EVEN IF SOME THOUGHT IT WAS TABOO.

DAILY THE QUEEN WOULD TIE ON HER SCARF,
THEN PLUNK ON HER CROWN,
TO GO FOR A MORNING SPIN AROUND TOWN.
AND IF SHE SAW SOMEONE WEARING A FROWN?
SHE'D STOP AND TELL A SILLY JOKE TO,
HELP TURN THEIR DAY AROUND.
AND IT HAS BEEN SAID,
WHEN SHE DROVE, HER FOOT WAS MADE OF LEAD.
THE QUEEN SPED? SHE GIGGLED.
CLEARLY PEOPLE HAD BEEN MISLEAD.

THE QUEEN HAD TWO CHILDREN, A GIRL AND A BOY.

THE LOVE THEY BROUGHT HER,

SHE FOUND NO GREATER JOY.

BUT AS ALL CHILDREN DO THEY GREW UP AND

MOVED AWAY.

LEAVING THE QUEEN ALONE,

WITH NO ONE TO PLAY.

NO BALL GAMES. NO CHEERS.

THINGS SHE'D LOOKED FORWARD TO,

OVER THE YEARS.

NO KIDS CLIMBING THE TOWERS.

NO ONE STOMPING ON ALL HER FLOWERS.

NO MUSIC OR MOVIES PLAYING ALL THROUGH THE NIGHT.

NO FEATHERS FLOATING ALL OVER AFTER A PILLOW FIGHT.

NO CRAZY ALL NIGHT SLEEP-OVERS,

WHERE THE PUPPY ALWAYS GOT UNWANTED MAKEOVERS.

THE QUEEN'S SON WAS ENGAGED.

HER DAUGHTER HAPPILY WED.

BOTH OF THEM LIVED IN HOUSES MADE OF GINGERBREAD.

THE UPKEEP MAKING THEM

WISHED THEY'D USED BRICK INSTEAD.

THINKING THEY WERE SLICK,

CHILDREN WOULD STROLL BY AND BREAK OFF A BRICK,

THEN TRY TO EAT IT LICKETY SPLIT...

ONLY TO MAKE THEIR TUMMIES FEEL SICK.

HER MAJESTY'S LONELINESS WAS KNOWN
THROUGHOUT HER DOMAIN.
SO A BALL WAS HELD TO EASE HER PAIN.
THE BUTCHERS, THE BAKERS, THE FANCY-SCHMANCY PIE MAKERS.
EACH GAVE HER THE MOST SUCCULENT TREATS.
AND BY GOD, EACH CONFECTION THE QUEEN DID EAT...
UNTIL HER BELLY PUFFED OUT SO MUCH
SHE COULD NO LONGER SEE HER FEET.

THE MUSICIAN PLAYED.

AND SOME MORE THAN OTHERS DANCED AND SWAYED.

THE ENTIRE NIGHT SEEMED HEAVEN-MADE.

THE KING SANG HIS QUEEN A LOVELY SONG,

AND EVEN THOUGH HIS TONE WAS ALL WRONG,

THE BALLAD DRONED ON AND ON.

EVERYONE JOINED IN AND SANG ALONG,

MAKING EACH PERSON THERE FEEL THEY BELONGED.

THE DOG THOUGH, HE COVERED HIS EARS...

FEARING HIS HEARING WOULDN'T BE RIGHT FOR YEARS.

THE PRINCESS SURPRISED THE QUEEN WITH A PLAYFUL DOG,

WHO WORE A PINK POUFY TUTU,

AND TURNED OUT TO BE A GIANT BED HOG.

HER PRINCE CAUGHT HER A FROG,

WHO LOVED TO SIT ON HER SHOULDER WHEN SHE WENT FOR A JOG.

RUNNING ONE DAY THE QUEEN FOUND A CAT.

FLUFFY, SOME MAY HAVE CALLED FAT.

THE CAT BESTOWED THE QUEEN WITH A RAT,

WHO SLEPT CURLED UP INSIDE THE QUEEN'S CROWNED HAT.

SHE WAS NOT TOO HAPPY ABOUT THAT.

IN THE PARK THE QUEEN WATCHED CHILDREN LAUGH AND BE GAY.

SHE WANTED GRANDCHILDREN IN THE WORST WAY.

WITH THAT THERE WASN'T MUCH SHE COULD
SAY, OTHER THAN PRAY, SOME DAY...

WITH THE DOG ON THE LEASH, THE CAT IN HER ARMS, THE FROG
ON HER SHOULDER, AND THE RAT NESTLED UNDER HER HAT,

THE QUEEN SWATTED AT A PESKY GNAT.

NOT MUCH SHE COULD DO ABOUT THAT,

EXCEPT TELL IT TO SCAT,

BEFORE THE TINY NUISANCE WENT SPLAT.

THE BOLD LITTLE GNAT LANDED SQUARELY ON HER NOSE,

AND STRUCK A POSE. ALL THAT WAS MISSING WERE LITTLE LEDERHOSEN.

THE QUEEN'S PEOPLE NOTED HER LOVE OF PETS,

AND BEGAN TO LAVISH HER WITH DIFFERENT ANIMALS IN SETS.

TWO GEESE. TWO LIONS. TWO TIGERS. TWO BEARS.

THEY TOOK OVER THE CHAIRS, SUNBATHED ON THE STAIRS.

AND FOR THE LOVE OF GOD THE PET HAIR,

WAS FOUND EVERYWHERE.

DUST BUNNIES GALORE.

TRYING TO KEEP UP WITH IT PROVED QUITE THE CHORE.

PAW PRINTS DECORATED THE FLOOR.

MEGA TRIPS TO THE STORE,

FOOD. THE ANIMALS WANTED MORE AND MORE.

TWO OWLS. TWO GOATS. TWO HORSES. TWO SHEEP.

THE QUEEN CONSIDERED HIRING A LITTLE
GIRL SOME CALLED MISS BO PEEP,

JUST SO SHE COULD GET SOME SLEEP.

TWO COWS. TWO ELEPHANTS. TWO PIGS.

THE QUEEN NEEDED NEW DIGS.

DUCKING TO GET IN CAME TWO GIRAFFES.

THE QUEEN AND HER STAFF DID NOTHING BUT LAUGH.

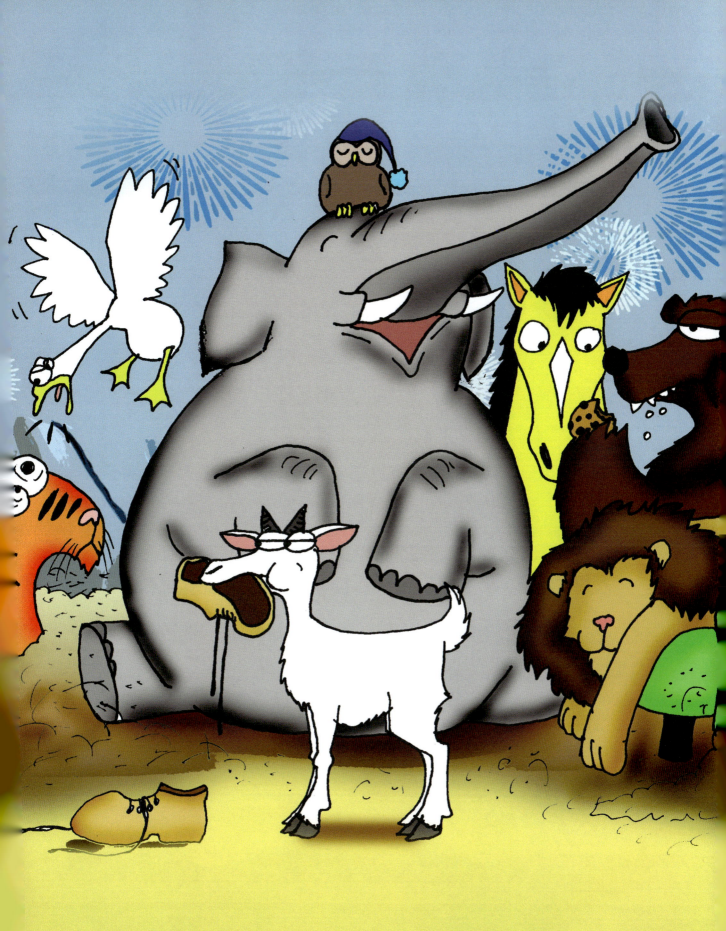

THE LAST TO ARRIVE WADDLED IN A PAIR OF AARDVARKS.
THAT SETTLED IT. THE TIME HAD COME TO EMBARK,
TO GET ALL THE ANIMALS TO A SAFE PARK,
AND TO DO IT THE QUEEN HAD TO BUILD AN ARK.
JIFFY QUICK, THE QUEEN HIRED A CREW,
WHO KNEW EXACTLY WHAT TO DO.
AFTER ALL, THEY BUILT A HOME FOR SOME,
OLD LADY WHO ACTUALLY LIVED IN A SHOE,
WITHOUT TOO MUCH TO-DO.
IN THE MEAN TIME THE CASTLE LOOKED MORE LIKE A ZOO...
AND THE SMELL...PEE-YEW!!!!

THE QUEEN AND HER FAMILY GATHERED FOR CHRISTMAS EVE.

HER FAVORITE HOLIDAY FOR IN SANTA SHE BELIEVED.

THE TABLE SET, THE CASTLE DECORATED,

HER LOVED ONES AROUND, THEY CELEBRATED.

DURING DINNER THE PRINCESS HANDED THE QUEEN A SPECIAL CHRISTMAS CARD.

WHEN THE QUEEN READ IT ALOUD…

SHE WAS THROWN COMPLETELY OFF GUARD.

FOR IN IT READ:

IN A FEW MONTHS YOU'LL SEE, A GRANDMA YOU'LL BE.

WHEN THE QUEEN'S LITTLE PRINCE GRACED THE EARTH WITH HIS BIRTH, THEY NAMED HIM NOAH. HIS NAME MEANT PEACE AND REST.

THEIR FAMILY HAD TRULY BEEN BLESSED.

WHEN NOAH TURNED ONE,

THE ARK WAS DONE,

THE QUEEN AND NOAH BOARDED THE SHIP,

COMPLETELY EXCITED ABOUT THEIR TRIP.

THE ANIMALS WOULD LIVE HAPPILY EVER AFTER
IN THEIR OWN, HOME SWEET HOMES.

JUST AS THE QUEEN DID WITH HER KING,
HER CHILDREN AND HER NOAH...

AND THE DOG AND THE FROG,

AND THE CAT AND THE RAT...

AND YES, EVEN THE PESKY GNAT.

Made in the USA
Charleston, SC
31 October 2015